D1580444

Anne Digby

Three R Detectives

THE SILLY POSTMAN MYSTERY

Illustrated by Gavin Rowe

STRAW HAT

First published in 1995 by Straw Hat

Text copyright © Anne Digby, 1995
Illustrations copyright © Gavin Rowe 1995

The moral right of the author has been asserted

Cover design by Expressive Design, Yeovil
Typesetting by Dragoman, London N16
Printed and bound in Great Britain
by WBC Ltd., Bridgend
for the publisher,
Straw Hat, Cambridge

A CIP catalogue record for this book is available from the British
Library

ISBN 1-899587-00-4

Contents

*Look very carefully
at every picture marked
with this sign. See if you
can solve the mystery before the Three Rs do!*

Chapter One

The Special Birthday

'Come on, Rose!' said Rupert.

'What are you doing?' asked Richie.

Rose was sitting at the kitchen table, carefully addressing an envelope.

The boys had come to her house to call for her. The Three Rs always walked to the village school together. Rose was usually ready first. But today she was last.

'I've got to get something in the post!' she explained. 'It's something really special. Look - '

5

She eased it out of its envelope.

It was a home-made birthday card.

Rose had drawn a huge *60* on the front with lots of little flowers climbing round and peeping through. She had coloured all the flowers brightly with crayons and stuck some gold glitter on them. The glitter made the petals shine. The card looked very pretty.

'Hey, that's good,' said Richie.

'All your own work?' asked Rupert.

'Yes. I made it last night. It took me ages. It's my gran's birthday tomorrow. That's why I've got to post it on the way to school.'

'A special card for a special birthday?'

'Yes, Rupe. Really special!'

'Here's your stamp, Rose,' said her mother, coming into the kitchen. 'And here's the other card, Daddy's and mine. Don't you dare forget to post them at Fox's Green! Granny's birthday will be spoiled if they don't arrive on the proper day.'

'As if I'd forget!' protested Rose.

They always passed the pillar box at Fox's Green on the way to school.

'Even if we miss the morning collection, there's still the afternoon one,' said Richie.

'I'm afraid the afternoon post won't do at all, Richie,' laughed Rose's mother. 'It might be too late. The cards have such a long way to go that we *have* to get them away by first post! But there's plenty of time.'

As the Three Rs set off for school, Rupert and Rose couldn't resist teasing Richie.

'First post doesn't go till ten o' clock, Rich,' said Rupert. 'I'm surprised you've never made a note of that!'

Richie was always mad about collecting information.

'Pete will only just have finished *delivering*,' Rose pointed out. 'Then he has his coffee break at his sister's. We see his van parked there, don't we?'

Mrs Kellaway's cottage was almost next door to the village school.

'Yes, but that could be *after* he's collected, for all I know,' said Richie, defensively.

'Never!' said Rose. She peeped into her school bag, just to make sure that the two cards were safe. It might rain soon.

Pete was their regular postman. Early each morning he drove out from the distant town of Kimbridge to bring the day's mail to their big, scattered village. It could take as long as two hours to deliver it all, driving up lanes to the clusters of houses; down rutted tracks to lonely farms.

He then enjoyed a good, long coffee break at Mrs Kellaway's before lifting the post from the village's three pillar boxes and taking it back to the sorting office in Kimbridge. In the afternoon he'd double back to make a second collection.

'First collection, ten o'clock. Second collection, half-past three. It's on the front of the Fox's Green pillar box,' said Rupert. 'You see it every time you post a letter!'

'I'm amazed you've never put it in your notebook, Richie!' laughed Rose.

The Three Rs loved to play detective. Sometimes they solved real mysteries. They

9

were lucky to have Rupert, who was their great brain-box. He was *very* observant and he was good at making deductions. Richie was more of a plodder, though good at running and climbing and things like that. Rose was an expert at organising the boys. The three friends made an excellent team.

Now, as they turned into Bacon Lane, Richie slapped his notebook pocket.

'I only write down important stuff,' he said, on his dignity.

The lane was deep and shady. As they strolled along, Rose glanced up at the sky.

'Oh, I *hope* it's not going to rain!' she exclaimed. 'Miss Ramsey says we're going to the pond if it's fine!'

Class 3R liked Environmental Studies. Rupert upturned his face.

'It's raining already,' he announced, as a large raindrop plopped on his nose.

'Come on, we'd better hurry,' said Richie.

Suddenly the rain was pelting down! They started to run.

'We're going to get soaked,' puffed Rupert, pulling on his anorak hood.

'What a cloudburst!' exclaimed Rose. She was glad that Gran's cards were safely in the bag, keeping dry. 'Hey, I've just thought - '

The lane turned sharp right here, winding round the bottom of a very steep hillock. Rose pointed upwards, to the top of it. The high mound was crowned by a fence, a stile and the familiar green fingerpost. The public footpath over Mr Shaw's field! As well as being a short cut, it led past his barn.

'Let's go up over the top way!' she shouted. 'Then we can shelter in the barn!'

It would be worth getting their wellies

muddy today, just to get out of this rain.

'Race you there!' yelled Richie.

He climbed fast and sure-footed up the steep incline. The other two floundered below, grabbing at tufts of grass to help them up the slippery slope.

'Bet Richie's in the barn, already!' puffed Rose.

But she was wrong.

Richie was standing up on the fence, above the stile, frozen like a statue.

'What's up with you?' asked Rupert.

'Come on!' said Rose, trying to push him.

'No. Wait a minute. Climb up here!' said Richie. 'I want you to see something!'

As they joined him, he pointed across the big field. The footpath led diagonally past the barn, to another stile in the far corner, and came out near the pillar box on Fox's Green.

Beyond that distant stile, they could see the gleam of a bright red metal van.

'Who says Pete always lifts the post at ten o' clock?' he asked. '*He's doing it now!*'

Through the curtain of rain they saw that the small red van was parked near the pillar box. The back doors of the van were open, a pair of navy-blue-trousered legs showing below. Pete was obviously round at the back of his van, getting out his mailbag.

'It's not allowed!' exclaimed Rose, in a panic. 'It's not even nine o'clock yet!'

'Quick, Rose, give me your bag,' said Richie. 'I'll try and catch him!'

Richie jumped from the top of the fence, into the field. He charged away along the footpath. Rupert and Rose followed, running their fastest. Nobody cared about sheltering from the rain any more. Richie had passed the barn now and was out of sight...

Gran's birthday cards, thought Rose, in despair. *Please catch the post in time, Richie.*

Chapter Two
A Very Silly Postman

'Did you catch him, Richie?' Rose cried out when she reached Fox's Green.

'Don't be silly, Rose,' said Rupert, who was right behind her. He was still clambering over the stile. 'Does it *look* like it?'

Richie was just a few paces away, leaning against the pillar box. He was still getting his breath back after his mighty run. His head was bowed. He looked the picture of dejection.

The other two joined him by the pillar box.

Richie handed Rose her bag back.

'Sorry, Rose. He'd gone.'

They stood looking up and down the road, this way and that. Just to make sure. But there was no sign of a little red post van.

'He'll be at Stump's Cross pillar box by now,' said Richie gloomily. 'And then on his way back to Kimbridge.'

The three friends gazed at one another. The heavy rain had stopped as suddenly as it had started. It was just a light drizzle now, with a hint of brightness in the sky. Rose pushed some hair out of her eyes. She was close to tears.

'It's not *allowed*,' she said, angrily. 'Pete's not allowed to lift the post an hour early. It's silly. Today of all days!'

She opened her bag and looked at the birthday cards.

'What shall I do now?' she asked helplessly.

'Post them, of course,' said Rupert, sensibly. 'What else can you do?'

Rose nodded. She took the cards out of her bag. Her heart felt heavy. As the two boys watched, she slowly pushed them into the mouth of the pillar box.

'Come on,' she said, dully. 'Let's get going.'

The three of them turned away from the pillar box and started to trudge up Fox's Hill.

'They might still get there,' said Richie, trying to cheer Rose up. 'There's still the number two post. It's okay sometimes ...'

Rupert, just in front of them, stopped dead in his tracks. It was so sudden that Rose and Richie bumped into him

'Hey, that's funny!' he exclaimed.

'Watch out, Rupe!' protested Richie.

'What's funny?' asked Rose.

'The pillar box!' said Rupert, turning round.

He went racing back to it. The other two followed him. What was this about?

The three Rs stood in front of the pillar box once more and stared.

'Well,' said Rupert. 'Notice anything?'

'It's red,' said Richie, just to be difficult.

'Look at the number,' said Rupert. 'The number of the next collection.'

'Oh, it still says *1*, ' realised Rose. 'How silly. It should say *2*.'

'It's strange,' said Rupert. 'It's peculiar that Pete should collect an hour early. And even more peculiar that he should *forget to change the number.'*

Rose felt a sudden glimmer of hope.

'Perhaps we made a mistake. Perhaps we just thought we saw the van parked here. Maybe Pete just paused a minute, on his way to Mrs Kellaway's.'

'Never,' said Richie. He walked to the spot where the van had been parked, near to Fox Cottage. 'We didn't make a mistake and this proves it.'

As the other two walked over, Richie already had pencil and notebook out. He was crouching down, examining the pattern of a tyre tread in the mud. It looked very fresh.

'A tyre impression, quite a deep one,' observed Rupert. 'Distinctive diamond patterned tyre.'

'From the post van,' said Richie. 'Pete parked here all right. We saw him, anyway - at the back of the van. I'll just copy this tyre pattern into my notebook.'

'Oh, Richie, whatever for?' asked Rose, crossly. Her flicker of hope had died. 'The stuff you put in your notebook. We'll be late for school at this rate.'

Doggedly Richie made the sketch in his notebook, all the same.

'I still don't see the point!' said Rose, when the Three Rs continued on their way

up Fox's Hill. 'What's the tyre tread got to do with it? Even though it wasn't our fault, we missed the post. That's that.'

'But at least my notebook *proves* it wasn't our fault!' said Richie. 'If your mum and dad try to blame you, we can show them the notebook and ...' he trailed off. 'Well, if anyone wanted to report Pete, it would be evidence,' he finished, lamely.

'Nobody's going to report Pete just for making one mistake,' said Rose, scornfully. 'Mum and Dad would never do that.'

Rupert had been saying nothing. He had been looking very thoughtful.

'Stop talking, you two,' he said. 'Let's try and make some sensible deductions. It's good detective practice. For a start it wasn't just one mistake, it was *two*. So what do we deduce from that? I mean it's not like Pete, is it?'

'Maybe - er - maybe he's got some big problem on his mind,' suggested Richie. 'Yes, that could be it!'

'I know!' suggested Rose. 'Maybe there's a new postman on today. Maybe it wasn't

Pete at all. And the new postman is just learning the ropes - '

'Yes,' agreed Rupert. 'That's exactly what I've deduced. In fact, it's got to be the answer.'

'I suppose it *could* explain things,' nodded Richie. 'But I still think my theory's quite good.'

None of this was much comfort to Rose.

'I'm going to make another deduction,' she said. 'I think there's a new postman on and whoever he is, he's a very silly one. And I hope we don't ever have him again.'

But when they reached the top of Fox's Hill and turned the corner -

'Hey, you two! Your theory's wrong!' exclaimed Richie. 'There's not a new postman on!' He pointed.

Pete's van was parked in its usual place at the side of Mrs Kellaway's cottage!

Rupert and Rose looked at each other in

surprise. But the school bell was ringing. They were late! They all ran towards the school gates.

As they rushed past the cottage, they caught a glimpse of Pete sitting in there, near the front window. It was him, all right. He was laughing away as he talked to his sister.

'Your theory's wrong too, Richie!' shouted Rupert as the three of them hurtled through the school gates. 'Pete didn't look to me as if he had some big problem on his mind.'

'I'm the one who's got that,' said Rose. It made her feel cross to have seen Pete looking so cheerful. 'He just decided he wanted to collect the post early, then. How silly!'

'But he's not usually silly, is he?' said Rupert, frowning.

'No, he isn't,' agreed Richie. 'It's all very baffling.'

Chapter Three
A Proper Mystery

If it weren't for Rupert being such a brain-box, Rose might have stayed cross with Pete the postman for ages. But Rupert was to come up with a brand new deduction - and a very clever one. This didn't happen straight away. First, there was a mad scramble not to be late for assembly.

'You held us up, Richie. You and your tyre marks!' said Rose, as they changed out of muddy wellies into indoor shoes and hung their wet anoraks up. The pegs were by the cloakroom radiator. With luck, the anoraks would be dry by playtime. 'You nearly made us late!'

It was all such a rush! There was no time to ponder the silly-postman mystery.

However, by the time she was sitting cross-legged on the floor in assembly, Rose's worries began to return. Mrs Keeping was playing a tinkling tune on the piano and there was the chance to think again.

Would the cards arrive on Gran's birthday? Or would they arrive a day late? Why did Pete have to collect from the box an hour early, today of all days? It wasn't allowed! It wasn't a bit like him, either.

Rupert was sitting next to Richie, at the end of the row. His brow was furrowed. He, too, was deep in thought.

After assembly, he had a whispered conversation with Richie. Then both boys grabbed hold of Rose.

'Cheer up!' hissed Richie. 'Rupe's had another idea. A really ace one. I don't know why we didn't think of it before!'

They were both smiling so broadly that Rose at once felt more cheerful.

'What?' she asked.

'Well, we know Pete *isn't* silly, don't we?' said Rupert, as they walked along the corridor to class 3R. 'So even if he had some special reason to collect the post early, he'd *never* forget to change the number, would he? So there's only one answer. It was just a coincidence that he was by the pillar box. He wasn't collecting. He was doing the opposite!'

'Like - ?' began Rose.

'Like *delivering* , of course!' burst in Richie. 'Just finishing his round. Aren't we stupid not to have thought of it?'

'Delivering something to Fox Cottage?' exclaimed Rose. She liked the sound of this idea. Nevertheless, she hesitated. 'But then why didn't we see his van on Fox's Hill?' she asked. 'Stopping off at the other houses, before he got to his sister's?'

'I've thought about that,' said Rupert. 'Look, he keeps the letters in the front of the van with him, doesn't he? But for some reason he'd had to go round to the back of the van. We saw him! So it must have been something special. Maybe a large parcel, that he was leaving till last. Or even forgotten about, because it was right at the very back of the van.'

Rose felt a weight lifting from her shoulders.

'Oh, Rupe. That's got to be it, hasn't it? So it means the first post hasn't been collected yet, after all?'

'Stop chattering, you three,' said Miss Ramsey, coming up behind them. 'You should be in the classroom by now.'

Richie gave Rose a friendly little push.

'Course it hasn't been collected!' he whispered. 'We've been worrying about nothing. Not a proper mystery at all, was it?'

'We haven't had one of those for ages,' said Rupert, looking quite disappointed.

He was speaking too soon.

* * *

'Thank goodness it's stopped raining,' said Rose, at playtime. 'Only just in time!'

Until five minutes ago, they had all feared

that the trip to the village pond was off.

In the second lesson Miss Ramsey, looking out of the window, had said to the class:

'Unless this rain stops very quickly now, I'm afraid we'll have to stay indoors today.'

There were lots of protests.

'We don't mind the rain, miss!'

'It's not proper rain. It's only drizzling.'

'Look, miss. I can see the sun trying to peep out. It's going to stop in a minute!' said one boy.

And he was right.

Hooray!

The Three Rs changed back into boots and anoraks and rushed out into the playground. Ten minutes for play. Then off to the village pond with Miss Ramsey. There were lilies floating on the dark green water there and lots of reeds and rushes. There were ducks. There was a moorhen. They would see her with her chicks today, Miss Ramsey said.

'Hey!' exclaimed Richie, suddenly. 'There's a police car outside.'

The Three Rs hurried across to the school gates and looked at it. The car was all locked up and parked on their wide, muddy verge. Richie looked at the number plate. It was the village's regular patrol car, usually driven by Police Constable Cork.

'I wonder what Mr Cork's come to school about?' he said, with interest.

'Let's go and find out,' said Rupert, turning round.

P.C. Cork was emerging from the school building with their headmaster. With them was Kevin, a big boy from 6B.

All three looked very solemn as they walked over to the bike shed.

'Come on! Let's try and listen!' suggested Rose.

A lot of others headed there, too. A small crowd was gathering. It seemed that Kevin's new mountain bike had been stolen!

He'd left it padlocked at school yesterday, when his mother collected him by car. They had both forgotten that he was going to the dentist after school.

This morning, the bike had gone!

'We're sure there's a gang at work,' the policeman told Mr Jones. 'Bikes have been going from all the villages lately. They probably have a pick-up truck and drive around after dark. They snatch the bikes, locks an' all, and take them back to base somewhere.'

He wrote a few things down in his notebook.

'I'll make some inquiries round the village, see if any other bikes were taken last night.'

Then he turned to the children.

'I want you all to keep your eyes open, youngsters. If you ever see or hear anything suspicious, tell your parents. Get them to ring the station straight away.'

The Three Rs looked at each other. Poor Kevin! But they were feeling quite excited. Just as Rupert was saying that they hadn't had a proper mystery for ages, here was a whopper.

As P.C. Cork left, they followed him out

through the school gates.

'Please, sir,' said Richie.

'Yes?' He was climbing back into his patrol car.

'We're good at solving mysteries. Can you tell us what kind of truck to look out for?'

The policeman leaned out of the window and laughed.

'Listen, young detective. If we could tell you that, we'd have picked it up by now!'

He drove away, leaving Richie hot cheeked.

'You asked for that!' grinned Rupert.

Richie frowned. He got his notebook and pencil out and started to scan the verge.

'There's loads of tyre marks. The truck must have parked somewhere along here. I'll sketch a few. And keep my eyes open for big 'uns.'

He crouched down and started copying

tyre patterns into his notebook.

'Rose and I'll look, as well,' said Rupert.

Rose and Rupert wandered up and down the muddy verge.

'Yes, the truck would have parked along here last night,' mused Rupert. 'While someone ran in and snatched the bike.'

'What good are the tyre marks, though?' asked Rose. Not tyre marks again! 'They won't tell us anything.'

'Oh, they might tell us a lot,' said Rupert. 'The size. The pattern of them. Distance between front and rear axle. Tell us what size the truck is, anyway.'

They both scanned the ground.

'Can't see anything unusual,' said Rupert. 'Trouble is the ground's all churned up after the heavy rain.'

'And everyone being brought to school by car!' agreed Rose. There were mashed up tyre marks everywhere. Car ones. 'I don't think we're going to find anything, Rupe.'

They wandered back to Richie. He was putting his notebook back in his pocket, looking disappointed.

'Find anything, Rich?'

'Only - '

Richie got no further because at that moment there came a loud whistle blast.

It was time to go to the village pond.

Chapter Four
The Bone Dry Clue

'And what have you three been up to?' asked Miss Ramsey. 'You know you're not allowed to go outside the school gates!'

The rest of the class had lined up in the playground. The Three Rs had tried to sneak back in, unseen. It would be so useful sometimes to be invisible! It would make being detectives so much easier.

Rose looked as meek as possible.

'We just wanted to ask Mr Cork something,' she said.

'We want to help find Kev's bike,' explained Rupert.

'We've been looking for clues!' added Richie.

Miss Ramsey shook her head and smiled.

'I might have guessed. Well, Three R Detectives, please join on to the back of the line. It's time to go.'

Their teacher was teasing them. But the rest of the class knew what good detectives they were.

'Richie, did you find anything?' asked one of the girls at the back.

Miss Ramsey was leading the procession out through the school gates now.

'Not yet,' replied Richie.

The long crocodile marched in the direction of Fox's Hill. Soon they were passing Mrs Kellaway's cottage. Miss Ramsey was a long way ahead, at the front. The Three Rs were at the very back.

They paused by the cottage for a moment. They looked at the driveway. Rose pointed to the place where Pete's post van had stood.

'He's gone,' she said, looking pleased. 'Gone to empty the pillar boxes. I expect he's on his way back to Kimbridge by now.'

'With your gran's birthday cards safely in the van!' said Richie. 'Bet you anything.'

Rose and Richie caught the others up.

Suddenly they realised that Rupert wasn't with them. Looking back, they saw him. He was still standing by Mrs Kellaway's, staring at the driveway.

Richie jumped up and down, waving and signalling.

'Come on, Rupe!' he hissed.

Rupert looked round, like someone in a trance. Then, running hard, he soon caught up with them.

'Did you notice something?' he whispered.

He was looking very, very puzzled.

'No, what?' asked the other two.

'The patch where the van had been standing. It was *completely dry*. But how could it be?'

They all frowned as they continued to march down the hill.

'I think I get you,' said Richie, slowly.

'So do I,' Rose nodded. 'What can it mean?'

'Let's take it step by step,' said Rupert. 'The ground under the van was bone dry. Right? That means Pete only left a few minutes ago, *after* it had stopped raining. Nothing odd about that. What's really odd is that.....'

'It must have been dry when he got there, too!' finished Rose.

'Exactly,' agreed Rupert. 'When we were caught in that downpour, he was *already at his sister's !'*

'So it couldn't have been *Pete's* van we saw across the field!' finished Richie. 'There *was* another postman on.'

'There must be two postmen on this morning!' gasped Rose.

'I've never seen that before,' said Rupert.

Rose felt a flutter of alarm. There was a silly postman, after all! One who collected

41

the post much earlier than he was supposed to. And didn't bother to change the number on the box.

They had reached the bottom of Fox's Hill and Miss Ramsey was seeing the class across the road. The Three Rs were the last to cross. As soon as they were over, their teacher hurried forward again to the head of the crocodile. She started to lead the class past Fox Cottage, past the pillar box and towards the green.

'Quick! Let's run and look at the pillar box!' Rose blurted out, anxiously.

The three of them jumped away from the end of the crocodile and raced past some of the tail-enders. Everybody was trampling over the place where the tyre mark had been.

'Yes! The pillar box!' said Rupert, his eyes bright with interest.

Ahead of them, Miss Ramsey was disappearing round the corner, marching the class on to Fox's Green. The village pond lay out of sight, beyond some trees on the other side of the green.

The Three Rs reached the pillar box and stared at it.

'Oh, thank goodness!' said Rose.

The number had been changed.

The *1* had gone. There was a *2* there now.

'The post *hadn't* been collected earlier. Look, someone's changed the number!' she said, in relief.

Gran's birthday cards were safely on their way!

But the boys were scratching their heads and looking puzzled.

'I don't get it,' said Richie. 'If that other postman hadn't driven out from Kimbridge to do the pillar boxes, what else was there for him to do?'

'I agree,' said Rupert. 'If it was just a new postman, learning the round, he'd have been with Pete. They'd have been together in the same van!'

Rose screwed her eyes up tightly. She was trying to see a picture in her mind.

'Perhaps it wasn't a postman at all!' she said.

'What d'you mean?' asked Richie. 'What are you closing your eyes for, Rose?'

'I'm trying to remember something. I'm trying to get a picture back. A picture of that van we saw across the field.'

'*Can* you see it, Rose?' asked Rupert, eagerly. 'I've been trying to remember, as well. But I just can't!'

Rose still had her eyes closed. She was concentrating very hard. She was good at getting memory pictures.

'It was bright red, exactly like a post van,' she murmured. 'And it had stopped near the pillar box. And ... it was the right shape. We were sure it was Pete's van. But it was miles away, and we were looking through the rain .... And ....' She opened her eyes wide. She looked startled.

'I've just seen it in my mind!' she exclaimed. She clapped her hands. 'It *didn't have any words on the side, like a real post van would.* It was just a plain red van. I'm positive!'

'So the man in dark blue trousers, round the back - ?' began Richie.

'Wasn't a postman at all!' said Rupert. 'Just someone pretending. Rose guessed right!'

The Three Rs stared at one another in excitement. Although they still couldn't piece the jigsaw together, they knew that they were on to something.

The whole class had gone by. The last two stragglers had just walked past them.

'What's so good about a pillar box?' they asked.

'Come on, you three! Hurry up! You'll get told off!'

'Tell Miss Ramsey we'll be along in a

minute!' said Rupert.

'We can't tell her that! She'll want to know what you're doing!'

'You just tell her!' rapped Richie. He knew that look in Rupert's eye. 'Tell her we won't be long but it's something really important!'

Their two classmates ran off, to catch up the rest.

'It had better be!' they shouted back. 'Or you won't half get into trouble!'

Chapter Five
Rupert's Brainwave

'Let's take another look at that tyre mark,' said Rupert.

They crossed the driveway of Fox Cottage, to look at the muddy verge again.

'The tyre mark's gone,' said Rose. 'It's just about wiped out.'

She was feeling a bit scared about not being with the class. She hoped Rupert knew what he was up to.

'Everybody trampled over it just now, that's why,' Richie was saying. 'But I've got a sketch of it, remember?'

The other two looked over his shoulder as he flicked through the pages of his notebook.

'You've got *two* sketches of it, Rich!' observed Rupert.

Richie had flicked over to the latest page.

'The van was up at the school sometime!' exclaimed Rose. 'Look! It's one of the tyre marks you sketched just a few minutes ago, at playtime. The same diamond pattern!'

'I know,' said Richie, airily. 'I was going to show you. But it didn't seem important. I mean, Pete would have to pull in there, wouldn't he, to deliver the school post this morning....'

'Except we now know it *wasn't* Pete's van,' said Rupert.

'And so it *is* important,' added Rose. 'Oh, Richie, your notebook's really brill! We're getting somewhere at last! We know a fake postman was driving round the village in a red van this morning - '

'And now we have proof that he parked by the school. Probably quite early,' deduced Rupert, 'before anyone got to school!'

'Don't you see, Richie,' prodded Rose. 'When Kev got to school this morning, his bike had gone. The police think it's a gang, going round at night. Maybe with a big truck. But suppose it's just one man, going round in broad daylight - '

'In a small red van!' gasped Richie. He was a bit slow sometimes but he always got there in the end. Now he flicked the pages of his notebook, backwards and forwards, checking. Yes, same tyres all right. 'If we're right, we've got the evidence!' he said excitedly. 'Right here in my notebook.'

'It's ace, Richie,' said Rupert, abstractedly. He wasn't looking at the notebook any more. He was gazing around and seemed very thoughtful.

'Yes. So many bikes have gone, the police think the crooks work at night, with some kind of truck. But one man in clothes that look like a postman's, driving round in a red van, could pinch loads of bikes!'

'It gives him the excuse to nip into people's gardens,' Rose added. 'Anyone driving past wouldn't notice. They'd just think it was a postman!'

'Like we did!' agreed Richie.

'Should we go and tell Miss Ramsey?' asked Rose. She was getting rather restless again. 'She'll be mad at us if we don't turn up soon!'

'No, wait,' said Rupert. 'There's something that's still puzzling me. What was a fake postman doing, stopping by a *real* pillar box? It doesn't make sense.'

He glanced at Fox Cottage's garage. Its doors were firmly shut. They'd been open on the way to school this morning.

Then he whistled in excitement. He walked slowly up the drive, bending his head to stare at the damp tarmac. He was looking at a long, faint, wiggly mark.

'Quick!' he said, as he came running back. 'We've got to go and knock at Mrs Marlow's front door!'

'Whatever for, Rupe?' asked Rose, anxiously. 'We'll be ever so late for the lesson.'

'I've had a brainwave! That's what for!'
he said, racing towards the garden gate of
Fox Cottage.

Rose followed him, suddenly reading his
mind. It took Richie a little longer. He gazed
blankly at the drive.

Then it dawned on him, too.

'Can I help you?' asked Mrs Marlow, as she opened her front door. A tiny girl, little more than a toddler, was peeping round her mother's legs. 'Say hello to the visitors, Harriet.'

But the tiny girl, holding on tight to her teddy bear, was too shy to speak.

She stared with big round eyes at the three visitors who were standing on her mother's doorstep.

'We're sorry to disturb you,' said Rupert politely. 'We were wondering if you keep a bike in your garage. And whether it's safe or whether it's gone missing.'

'Yes, I do keep a bike in the garage,' smiled Mrs Marlow. 'It's a nice new one. But it certainly isn't missing! Not as far as I know!'

'Do you think we could just look and make sure?' asked Rupert.

'Whatever for?' asked the woman.

'Someone's been going round the villages stealing bikes,' explained Rose.

'We just ought to make sure!' added Richie.

'Ah! But we always keep the garage locked!' explained Mrs Marlow.

'It was open just before nine o' clock,' said Rupert, tactfully. 'We noticed, on our way to school.'

'Ah.' The woman thought for a moment. 'Well, yes. My husband opens it every morning. Just to get the car out and drive to work. But then I always come out and close it again. As soon as I've washed and dressed Harriet.'

She began to look anxious.

'I didn't really check - ' she said.

'D'you think it would be a good idea just to make sure?' repeated Richie, urgently.

'All right.' Mrs Marlow placed the toddler's hand in Rose's. 'Hold on to her while we go and get the doors opened up.'

She fetched the keys, then she led the Three Rs round to the garage. 'Hello, Harriet!' said Rose. 'What a smashing teddy bear. Shall we see what Mummy is doing?'

Mrs Marlow was easing open the garage doors. She peered inside.

Harriet held Rose's hand, her eyes very round, trying to follow what was going on.

Then Mrs Marlow emerged from the garage, looking upset. 'It's gone!' she exclaimed. 'My bike's been taken!'

The Three Rs stared at one another. And suddenly the little toddler by Rose's side found her voice.

'Mummy's bike!' she piped up. 'Silly postman! Silly postman got mummy's bike!'

'Ssh, Harriet!' said her mother. She was still looking shocked. But she came and took the toddler from Rose and held her close. 'You mustn't say things like that! Pete the

postman wouldn't steal mummy's bike.'

'Silly postman!' repeated the child.

'Ssh!' She put her finger over the child's lips and turned to the Three Rs. 'She always watches from her cot when Pete brings the post. She'll have seen him come to the house this morning. So, of course, she thinks it must be him!'

Mrs Marlow was looking very agitated now.

'Oh, my lovely new bike. Thank you for warning me. I'd better phone the police - '

'There's no need!' said Richie, staring up the road.

A police patrol car was cruising slowly along.

'Mr Cork's in the village right now. I'll go and wave him down!'

As Richie raced to the garden gate, Rupert turned to Mrs Marlow.

'Your little girl's dead right, you know! It wasn't Pete. But it really was a silly postman who took your bike. She must have seen him from her bedroom window!'

'I'm sorry? I don't understand - '

'We saw a red van with its back doors open,' Rose explained. 'We saw it right from the other side of Mr Shaw's field. We thought it was the postman, sorting through the mail. But it was a bike thief. He must have been loading your bike in, right at that very moment!'

She turned to Rupert.

'That was a great deduction, Rupe,' she said. 'What a brainwave!'

'It was that faint mark on the wet drive,' he replied, pointing. 'I was almost sure it was the remains of a cycle track. Leading from the garage to where the van was parked.'

'And you realised - '

'That maybe it wasn't the pillar box that the red van had stopped for! Maybe it was the sight of someone's ace bike in the garage, waiting to be pinched!'

Brain-box Rupert, right again.

Solemnly, he walked over and took the toddler's little hand in his.

'Shake, Harriet,' he said.

Chapter Six

Three Cheers for the Three Rs

They all went outside then, to the roadside. It was a great moment for Richie.

He had already waved down the police car. He was excitedly showing P.C. Cork the sketches in his notebook. He was telling him about the red van and about the second bike theft, from the garage.

'We've got an eye-witness, as well!' said Mrs Marlow, hugging her daughter. 'Little Harriet saw the man take it!'

'You'll soon have your bike back,

ma'am,' said the policeman. He was looking extremely pleased. 'We know exactly what to look for now. This is the big break we've been waiting for.'

He turned to Richie and patted his head.

'You and your friends have proved yourselves real detectives,' he said. 'And this notebook of yours contains important evidence, son.'

Richie went hot in the cheeks again. But this time it was with pleasure.

'What will you do now, sir?'

'Get in the car and I'll show you. Your friends, too. Now we've got an exact description of the vehicle, it won't get far. A bright red post-type van! It'll stick out like a sore thumb!'

It was thrilling for the Three Rs to be allowed to sit in the police car while P.C. Cork put out the radio alert.

Within minutes, every patrol car over a

wide area would be looking for a bright red van, postal size, no markings.

And when the 3R class monitors came to find them, saying that Miss Ramsey was very cross, the policeman just smiled.

'I'll bring them over to the pond myself,' he said. 'She won't be cross when she hears what I've got to say. She'll be very proud.'

'I think you're very clever young detectives,' said Mrs Marlow.

The rest of the morning was brilliant. It was lovely by the village pond. The sun came out from behind the clouds. The mother moorhen came out from behind the reeds. Her head jerked backwards and forwards like a clockwork toy, six little clockwork chicks bobbing along behind her.

One of the boys had brought a jam jar and managed to scoop up some frog spawn from the edge of the pond.

'We'll take it back with us and make a tiny pond at school,' Miss Ramsey promised the class. 'We'll watch the frog spawn turn into tadpoles and then into frogs.'

The afternoon was even more brilliant.

Just before the end of school, the headmaster came into Class 3R with Kevin. And P.C. Cork.

The policeman announced that the red van had been spotted in a village near Kimbridge and a man arrested. He was wearing dark clothes, very much like a postman's. Both Kevin's bike and Mrs Marlow's had been safely recovered. They were in the back of the van with two others.

'Come on, class!' said Miss Ramsey. 'I want us to give three cheers for Rupert, Rose and Richie.'

Everybody cheered very loudly. And Kevin clapped them warmly on the back.

For Rose, the best moment of all was when her gran phoned the house. It was the following evening.

'I don't know what to say, Rosie love. Your card is just beautiful. I think it's the best birthday card I've ever had. It was such a lovely surprise when it arrived this morning. I've been looking at it all day.'

'Happy birthday, Gran!' said Rose.